This is an Arthur A. Levine book
Published by Levine Querido

www.levinequerido.com · info@levinequerido.com

Levine Querido is distributed by Chronicle Books, LLC

Text and illustrations copyright © 2022 by Paula Cohen

Library of Congress Cataloging-in-Publication data is available
ISBN 978-1-64614-126-5

Printed and bound in China

```
        TM
 ✓           MIX
             Paper from
             responsible sources
FSC          FSC™ C104723
www.fsc.org
```

Published in March 2022
First Printing

Book design by Semadar Megged

The text type was set in Parango TF

The art for this book was created using pencil sketches which were then
over-drawn and colored digitally with Procreate.

BIG DREAMS, SMALL FISH

Paula Cohen

LQ
LEVINE QUERIDO
MONTCLAIR • AMSTERDAM • HOBOKEN

In memory of Shirley, Evelyn, and Joseph,
who enjoyed the best gefilte fish.

Shirley's family had big dreams for their new store in their new neighborhood.

Uncle Morris stocked the shelves and no one made a taller tower. Papa kept the store tidy and helped the customers.

Mama filled the pots with her specialties
and made the best noodle kugel.

But one specialty, no one would buy:
gefilte fish.

No one would even TRY it.

Shirley to the rescue!

She had LOTS
of big ideas.

How to make things faster,

prettier,

and more modern.

But first of all, nothing sold gefilte fish.

And besides, Shirley's family thought she was . . .

. . . too little to help.

Her father said, "We didn't come to this country for
you to solve problems. Go play nice with the cat."

Her mother said, "You're in the way, Shirley.
You're making me farmisht!!"

Then a miracle happened. Aunt Ida was having a baby and the adults had to rush to the hospital. But if they all left . . . "WHO would run the store?"

"Me me me!" said Shirley. "I'm ready for duty."

"Mrs. Gottlieb is here," said Uncle Morris, "And Shirley can help."

Papa gave Shirley a kiss on
the keppele.
"Sell the fish or we'll be
eating it for weeks!" said Papa.

Mama said, "Don't worry about selling.
The neighbors don't know from good gefilte fish.
Just mind Mrs. Gottlieb."

"I'm taking fish for Ida!" shouted
Uncle Morris. "NOW HURRY!"

When they were gone
Shirley wasted no time.

She straightened.

She decorated.

She modernized.

She advertised.

"What a masterpiece!"

Mrs. Hernandez arrived. "Tomatoes please, Shirley, and a pound of noodle kugel."

Shirley packed up her order
nicely and placed a special surprise
inside the bag.

Mr. Lombardo came next. "Tuna please,
Shirley. Two tins for me. Two for the cats."
The Traub boys came with their list. And
Miss Han.

Later that evening, each neighbor found a surprise.

When Mama and Papa returned they found a surprise too.

"The gefilte fish is gone!
Shirley sold ALL of it!"
said Mama.

"But so little money in
the register!" said Papa.

"SURPRISE! I gave it all away!"
Mama was not happy. Papa was
furious. Shirley was sent to
bed early.

In the morning Shirley went
downstairs to roll up the blinds.

And there was Mrs. Hernandez. And Mr. Lombardo.
The Traub boys. Miss Han. The whole neighborhood.

All lined up. And all waiting for the
new neighborhood delicacy: gefilte fish.

"You know Shirley, you have some pretty
good ideas in that keppele after all," said Mama.
"That's my smart meydele," said Papa.

Shirley helped hang up
the new sign.

After all, it was
Shirley's store too!

And there was work to do!

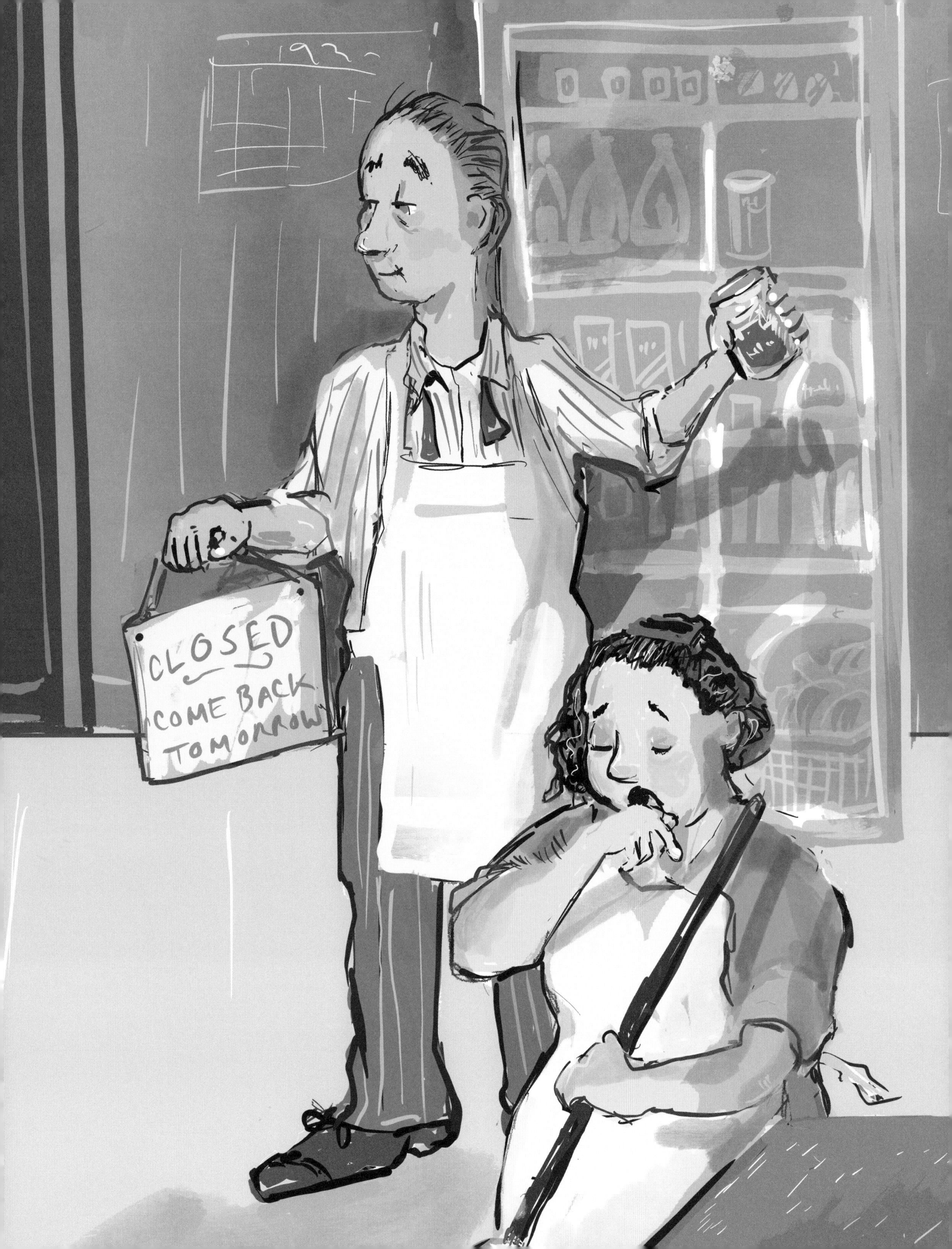
CLOSED
COME BACK
TOMORROW

Glossary

Some of the words in this book are Yiddish.

Yiddish is the language spoken by many Jews who emigrated from Eastern Europe. It is a combination of many languages including Hebrew, German, Polish and Russian.

Pitzele (pronounced Pits-eh-leh): Little one

Farmisht (pronounced Fuh-misht): Mixed up, confused

Keppele (pronounced Kep-eh-leh): Little head

Meydele (pronounced May-del-eh): Little girl

Gefilte Fish

Gefilte fish is a traditional Jewish dish made of ground fish (often a combination of carp, pike, and whitefish) mixed with matzoh meal (ground matzoh), eggs, and sometimes vegetables and spices. It can be baked or boiled. Gefilte means "stuffed" in Yiddish. The original recipes called for actually stuffing a fish! Later it became popular to make it into a patty (sort of like hamburger) which was served with a sliced carrot and a side of horseradish. Today some people form it into a loaf, like meatloaf, and serve it in slices. It can also be purchased in jars but make no mistake, homemade gefilte fish is very different and more delicious!

Serving gefilte fish was as a good way for new American immigrants to save money by making a fish or two stretch into several meals. It is said that this dish honors the Sabbath and brings blessings to those who eat it.

Russ Family Salmon and Whitefish Gefilte Fish

Gefilte fish is traditionally made with a combination of ground fish such as whitefish, carp, and pike. This recipe uses whitefish and salmon. These days, you can order pre-ground fish at some fish stores and grocers, but we recommend asking your local fish store to grind fresh salmon and whitefish for you, or putting it through a meat grinder at home. Failing that, you can cut the fresh fish into 1-inch pieces and put them in the freezer on a baking sheet for 15 minutes, then pulse in batches in a food processor—you want to chop finely, not make a paste. Your local fish store can be a source for fish stock, too. Or use fish bouillon cubes or fish base from the grocery store.

Makes 12

2 pounds salmon fillet, ground	4 1/2 teaspoons sugar
1 pound whitefish fillet, ground	1/4 teaspoon black pepper
1 large white onion, finely minced	1/2 cup coarsely ground matzoh meal
2 large eggs	3 quarts (12 cups) water
3 tablespoons chopped fresh dill	8 cups fish stock
2 tablespoons coarse kosher salt	Red horseradish for serving

1. In a large mixing bowl, combine the ground salmon and ground whitefish. One by one, add the onion, eggs, dill, salt, sugar, pepper, and matzoh meal, making sure to mix well after each addition. Cover with plastic wrap and refrigerate for 1 to 4 hours to allow the flavors to blend.

2. Divide the fish paste into 12 portions and shape into slightly flattened balls. Place them on a baking sheet lined with plastic wrap or parchment paper.

3. In a large stock pot, bring the water to a boil. Add the fish stock. When the liquid returns to a boil, turn the heat down to low. Use a slotted spoon to gently lower 6 of the fish balls into the stock. Once the gefilte fish rise to the surface, allow them to simmer for an additional 15 minutes. Using a slotted spoon, transfer the gefilte fish to a container large enough to hold them in one layer. Repeat with the remaining fish balls. Cool to room temperature, then cover and refrigerate until cold.

4. Slice the gefilte fish and serve cold with a dollop of red horseradish.

Adapted from the Russ & Daughters family recipe